More Than Enough

Written & Illustrated by

Stephanie A. Kilgore-White

DP KIDS PRESS

244 5th Ave, Suite G200
New York, NY 10001
(646) 233-4366
www.DocUmeantPublishing.com

More Than Enough
Charity Series, Vol 2, Bk 1

Published by
DP Kids Press
a division of DocUmeant Publishing
244 5th Avenue, Suite G-200
NY, NY 10001

646-233-4366

Digitally colored by Ginger Marks, DocUmeantDesigns.com

Scriptures taken from the Holy Bible, New International Version®, NIV®. Copyright © 1973, 1978, 1984, 2011 by Biblica, Inc.™ Used by permission of Zondervan. All rights reserved worldwide. www.zondervan.com The "NIV" and "New International Version" are trademarks registered in the United States Patent and Trademark Office by Biblica, Inc.™
ISBN: 9781957832104 (pbk)
ISBN: 9781957832111 (ePub)
Library of Congress Control Number: 2023943499

We live in a society where greed is dominating our culture. It has trickled down to our young children. They are in a competition to see if they can accumulate more and more stuff. We as parents have made it accommodating, with ease, to satisfy their every desire, thus cultivating a generation who struggles with greed. The more they see, the more they want. Bigger seems to be better. More is never enough.

If only, our young could see how truly blessed they are, not with more stuff, but with the bare necessities of life. If only they could take a trip to neighboring places where children are grateful to have a bite to eat, clean clothes to wear, and a place to lay their heads at night. Then, maybe then, would they show an attitude of gratitude, dismissing a desire to accumulate more unnecessary stuff.

For this reason, I dedicate this book to all the moms who are desiring to instill an attitude of gratefulness and contentment in their children. In Luke 12:14, Jesus tells us to be on guard against greed. We are to teach our children to appreciate their blessings and to also be a blessing to others in return.

"Someone in the crowd said to him, 'Teacher, tell my brother to divide the inheritance with me.' Jesus replied, 'Man, who appointed me a judge or an arbiter between you?' Then he said to them, 'Watch out! Be on your guard against all kinds of greed; life does not consist in an abundance of possessions'" (Luke 12:13–15).

Love and blessings!

My name is Ariel, and
I'm an only child.
I am lazy, spoiled, and
my life is quite wild.

There's nothing I want that I can't always get.
It has become a game to me I have to admit.

I enjoy searching the web for the latest new toys. Especially the popular items that others enjoy.

I like the challenge of being the first to get new things.
So I can brag to my friends, oh the jealousy it brings.

The only problem, however, is never being content. Which will often lead to a parental argument.

My parents have become very
concerned about me.
Because of my greed
which is apparent for all to see.

I never do my chores, nor do I help my parents out.

And when things don't go my way, I am quick to sulk and pout.

They tell me I'm ungrateful,
and do not appreciate,
The love and sacrifice they
constantly demonstrate.

Within a matter of time, Charity
shows up on the scene.
And I tell her how my parents are
awful and mean.

She affirms that I am loved and have
everything confused.
And I definitely have my parents
wrongfully accused.

Charity makes me aware that I have everything I need. And that over time I've developed an attitude of greed.

I'm now aware how God has blessed me with everything.

I have food, shelter, and clothing, not lacking anything.

I decide to share and give
to others in need.
This is definitely one way to
rid my life of all my greed.

I gather up some toys and
other items too.
And distribute them to others,
it's just the right thing to do.

From now on, I will share and
ask for only what I need.
And learn to be more grateful
to avoid a life of greed.

Words from the Author

I hope that you've enjoyed this book, but oh there's so much more. There will be others soon to come, featuring the character that you'll come to adore.

Charity wants to be your friend, you can introduce her to others too!

Join with me at my website, where you'll find out what's in store.

https://heavensdivinekiss.net/

If you have enjoyed this book, please let me hear from you. Also, be sure to leave a positive review on your favorite bookstore's website.

anne.white
.399488

stephan69239406

heavensdivine
kiss1377

hdkiss1377